THE SECRET OF THE HIDDEN

BOOK TWO

RACE TO THE ARK

BY M. J. THOMAS

For my mom and dad. Thank you for your love, sacrifices, and creativity.

—M.J.T.

ISBN: 978-0-8249-5685-1

WorthyKids
Hachette Book Group
1290 Avenue of the Americas
New York, NY 10104

Library of Congress Cataloging-in-Publication Data
Names: Thomas, M. J., 1969- author.
Title: Race to the ark / by M.J. Thomas.
Description: Nashville, Tennessee : WorthyKids/ideals, [2017] | Series: Secret of the hidden scrolls ; book 2 | Summary: "Peter, Mary, and their faithful dog Hank travel back to the time of Noah. With only seven days to solve the riddle of the scroll and escape the impending flood, Peter, Mary, and Hank must race to help Noah and his family finish the ark"-- Provided by publisher.
Identifiers: LCCN 2017021811 | ISBN 9780824956851 (paperback)
Subjects: | CYAC: Time travel--Fiction. | Noah (Biblical figure)--Fiction. | Noah's ark--Fiction. | Deluge--Fiction. | Scrolls--Fiction. | Brothers and sisters--Fiction. | Dogs--Fiction. | BISAC: JUVENILE FICTION / Religious / Christian / Action & Adventure.
Classification: LCC PZ7.1.T4654 Rac 2017 | DDC [Fic]--dc23 LC record available at https://lccn.loc.gov/2017021811

Cover illustration by Graham Howells
Designed by Georgina Chidlow-Irvin

Lexile® level 560L

Printed and bound in the U.S.A.
LSC-C

7 2020

CONTENTS

Prologue

Nine-year-old Peter and his ten-year-old sister, Mary, stood at the door to the huge, old house and waved as their parents drove away. Peter and Mary and their dog, Hank, would be spending the month with Great-Uncle Solomon.

Peter thought it would be the most boring month ever—until he realized Great-Uncle Solomon was an archaeologist. Great-Uncle Solomon showed them artifacts and treasures and told them stories about his travels around the globe. And then he shared his most amazing discovery of all—the Legend of the Hidden Scrolls! These weren't just dusty old scrolls. They were filled with secrets—and they would lead to travel through time.

Soon Peter, Mary, and Hank were flung back in time to the Creation of the earth. They saw amazing things and had exciting adventures, all while trying to solve the secret of the scroll.

Now Peter and Mary are ready for their next adventure . . . as soon as they hear the lion's roar.

1

THE RAIN

"Will it ever stop raining?" said Peter. He stared out of the window of Great-Uncle Solomon's house. It had been raining for two days. Peter wanted to go outside and explore the woods.

"*Ruff!*" barked Hank. He dropped a ball at Peter's feet.

"It's too wet to go outside," said Peter.

Hank picked up the ball and dropped it at Mary's feet. She didn't look up from the book she was reading.

"*Woof!*"

Hank barked so loudly, Mary almost jumped out of the comfy leather chair. Hank dropped the slobbery ball into her lap.

"Yuck!" She picked it up and threw it. It hit Peter in the back of the head.

"Ouch!" Peter rubbed his head. "Why did you do that?"

"Don't bother me," she said. "I'm reading."

Peter couldn't understand why Mary read so much. She read about history, science, animals, and space. It was almost like she *enjoyed* it.

"What are you reading?" asked Peter.

Mary held up the book. "*The History of Dogs: A Tale of Survival from the Bark Ages to Today.*"

"Sounds boring," said Peter. He threw the ball down the hallway. Hank brought it back.

"It's not." Mary showed them a picture of a wolf. "Did you know that Hank's great-great-great-great-great-grandfather was a wolf?"

Hank growled at the picture.

"Easy, Hank." Peter grabbed his collar so he wouldn't attack the book. "It's just a picture." Peter looked at the picture and then at Hank. "How could that mean-looking wolf be Hank's great-great-great-great-great-grandfather?"

"All dogs come from wolves," Mary said. She showed Peter a picture full of dogs. "In fact, there are more than 340 breeds of dogs that come from one wolf."

"*Wolf,*" barked Hank. He walked a little bigger and tougher around the living room. He even ran over and growled at the tall, shiny suit of armor guarding the hallway to the library.

The suit of armor didn't move.

"It's okay," said Peter. "It's not alive." He slowly reached his hand toward the armor but pulled back. "At least, I don't think it's alive."

Peter took a closer look. There was a long

sword in its right hand and a shield in its left. Peter backed away a bit.

"Hey, Mary!" shouted Peter. "Come look."

Mary grunted as she walked across the room. "What's so important?"

Peter pointed. "Do you remember seeing this lion on the shield?"

Mary bent forward. "I don't think so. Maybe it's a clue."

"A clue for what?" Peter asked.

"Maybe it's time to go to the library and open another scroll," said Mary. "It's been three days since we opened the first one."

Peter ran down the hall and slid to a stop in front of the library. The doors were tall and old and looked like they came from a castle.

He reached toward a handle. It was shaped like a lion's head.

"Open it!" Mary said.

Peter squeezed tight. "It won't turn."

Mary sighed. "I guess we'll have to wait for the lion's roar. Remember, the Legend of the Hidden Scrolls said, 'Amazing adventures are in store for those who follow the lion's roar.'"

"Too bad. Today would be a good day for an adventure," Peter said.

He looked down at Hank. "So what do you want to do now?"

Hank ran back down the hallway and brought the ball back.

Peter threw it again. It bounced off walls and rolled into a room. Hank chased it.

"Hank, come back!" shouted Peter.

Hank ran out of the room with a huge bone in his mouth.

"Drop it!" said Peter. "You don't know where that bone has been."

Hank wouldn't drop it.

"It could be from an old mummy," said Peter.

Hank dropped the bone and growled at it.

"Come on. Let's put it back before we get in trouble." Peter picked up the bone and began to walk down the hallway. He wondered when the lion would roar again so they could go in and open another scroll.

"Woof!"

He walked toward the doorway of the room. When he looked in, his mouth dropped open.

"Mary!" he shouted. "You've got to see this!"

2

An Old Leather Book

"Look what I found!" shouted Peter.

Mary sighed as she walked down the hallway.

"Hurry!"

"Okay, I'm here." Mary folded her arms. "Now, what is so important?"

Peter pointed into the room. Mary's eyes got as big as saucers.

"Look at all these shovels." Peter picked up a small shovel from a pile on the shelf. "We could have used this to build a sandcastle on our last adventure."

"This must be where Great-Uncle Solomon keeps his archaeology tools," said Mary.

Peter picked up some binoculars. "Check these out."

Peter looked across the room through the binoculars. When he turned back to Mary, she was unrolling a large map she had found on the table.

Peter grabbed a flashlight from a shelf. "What's that?"

"It's a map of Israel," said Mary.

"How do you know?" asked Peter.

Mary pointed to the top of the map. "It's written right there in big letters: Israel."

"I know," said Peter. "I just wanted to make sure you did."

Mary shook her head. "Sure you did."

Peter shined the flashlight on the map. "What is the big red X right in the middle?"

Mary picked up a magnifying glass from the table. "It looks like the X is on top of some hills in a desert beside the Dead Sea."

"Wait," said Peter. "Isn't that where Great-Uncle Solomon discovered the Hidden Scrolls?"

"You're right!" Mary looked up.

"I'm right sometimes," Peter said, grinning.

"I wonder if there's anything else here to help us find out more about the scrolls," said Mary.

"Woof! Woof!"

Hank was standing over a brown leather bag. Peter picked it up and plopped it on the table.

Mary gave Peter a big-sister look. "Be careful. We don't know what's in there."

Peter unzipped the bag and looked inside. "There's nothing here but an old leather book." He tossed it on the table.

Mary opened the book. "This isn't just a book. It's a handwritten journal."

"What's it about?" said Peter.

Mary looked down and read.

July 8th

It is very hot in this desert. Even my camel is getting thirsty. I have been searching for the Hidden Scrolls for 152 days, and I am losing hope of ever finding them.

"What else does it say?" Peter moved closer so he could see.

Mary turned the page.

July 9th

I hired a new guide today. He knows more about the scrolls than I do. He told me the scrolls were hidden 2,000 years ago, but he can help me find them. He also told me the Legend of the Hidden Scrolls. I am writing it down so I don't forget.

THE LEGEND OF
THE HIDDEN SCROLLS

The scrolls contain the
truth you seek.
Break the seal,

unroll the scroll,
and you will see the past unfold.
Amazing adventures are in store
for those who follow
the lion's roar!

"There you are," said a raspy old voice behind them. "I see you found my adventure journal."

Peter spun around. Great-Uncle Solomon was standing in the doorway. He adjusted his round glasses under his bushy white eyebrows.

Mary quickly closed the book and put it on the table. "Peter found it and made me read it."

Peter's heart pounded in his chest. "It's not my fault. Hank found it."

Great-Uncle Solomon smiled. "Don't worry. I'm not angry." He picked up the journal and flipped through the pages. "This journal has many great memories."

Roar!

The lion's roar echoed down the hallway from the library.

"There is no time to tell you!" said Great-Uncle Solomon. He ran around the room, grabbing things from the shelves and putting them in the brown leather bag.

"What are you doing?" asked Mary.

Great-Uncle Solomon put the journal in the bag and zipped it shut. "Here are a few things to help you on your adventure."

Roar!

"Go!" Great-Uncle Solomon handed the bag to Peter. "You don't want to make the lion wait."

"Let's go!" said Peter. He hung the

bag over his shoulder and ran down the hall to the library. Mary and Hank were close behind. Peter stopped and stared at the lion's-head handle. He reached for the handle and turned.

Click!

Peter swung the door open and they ran in.

Bang! The door shut behind them.

Roar! The sound came from behind the tall bookshelves on the right. Hank ran over and barked at one of the books.

Mary quickly found the red book with a lion's head painted in gold on the cover. She pulled it off the shelf. The tall bookshelf rumbled. Then it slid open to reveal the hidden room. It was dark, except for a glowing clay pot in the center of the room that held the scrolls.

Peter ran to the pot with Mary and Hank on his heels. Hank sniffed at one of the scrolls. Peter picked it up and looked at it.

"What's on the red wax seal?" Mary asked.

Peter took a closer look. "I'm not sure."

Mary looked at it. "I think it's a boat."

"I guess we could use one with all this rain," said Peter.

He broke the seal. Suddenly, the walls shook, books fell off the shelves, and the floor quaked.

Peter grabbed Mary's hand. "Here we go!"

The library crumbled around them and disappeared. Then everything was still and quiet.

3

Down in the Valley

Peter let go of Mary's hand and looked around. They were in the middle of woods. The sun shone through the branches and birds sang.

"At least it's not raining," said Peter. "Where are we?"

"It's hard to tell." Mary looked at the tall trees all around them. "These woods could be anywhere."

Peter pointed over her shoulder. "Let's go that way."

"No," said Mary. "This way."

Peter rolled his eyes. "Whatever. Let's just start moving. I'm getting hungry."

"Check the bag," said Mary. "Maybe Great-Uncle Solomon packed food."

Peter unzipped the bag and looked inside. He pulled out a flashlight and compass.

"Give me the compass," said Mary. "It will help keep us from getting lost."

Next, Peter pulled out a box of matches. "Who would give matches to a couple of kids?" Then he pulled out a hatchet.

"Be careful!" Mary gave Peter that look again.

Peter rolled his eyes and carefully laid the hatchet on the ground. He pulled out a small bag with a rope hanging out. He read the words on the bag. "Pop-up tent. Pull the rope and let your adventure begin." He grabbed the rope.

"Wait!" said Mary. "We might need that later. Is there anything else?"

Peter pulled out a canteen. "Water!" He opened it. "Empty!"

Finally, he pulled out Great-Uncle Solomon's adventure journal. "That's all. There's nothing to eat. We have to remember to bring food next time."

He shoved everything back into the bag, including the scroll.

Mary held up the compass. "Let's go north."

Peter led the way as they walked over fallen branches and rocks. About an hour later, they came to the edge of the woods. Peter stared down a steep hill into a valley.

A tall rock wall wrapped around a city filled with small houses and tiny gardens. A towering stone building shaped like a pyramid sat right in the center of the city.

"Civilization!" shouted Peter.

"Maybe we can find out where we are," said Mary.

Peter rubbed his belly. "Maybe we can find some food."

"*Woof!*" Hank barked and ran down into the valley.

Peter and Mary followed. At the bottom of the hill, Peter pointed to an iron gate. He opened it and followed Mary down a wide dirt road. The road was lined with shops that were filled with baskets, blankets, and jewelry. But Peter didn't see any food. He bumped into a tall, bearded man wearing a brown robe with a rope tied around his big, bouncy belly.

"Get out of my way!" grunted the man. He kicked dirt on Hank and pushed his way past Peter and Mary.

"Sorry," said Peter. He brushed the dirt off Hank.

People crowded the street. Everyone pushed and shoved and gave each other mean looks. There were no hellos, no handshakes, and no smiles.

"We still need to find food," said Peter.

Mary agreed with him, for once. She and Hank followed Peter as he pushed his way through the smelly, cranky crowd. Nobody looked happy. Peter thought they must be hungry too. Where was the food?

Suddenly he smelled something. It wasn't a familiar smell, like hot dogs or pizza, but he was pretty sure it was food.

Peter let his nose lead him to a large outdoor food shop. There he found baskets full of fresh bread.

Mary found tables covered with bananas, oranges, and apples. And Hank found a shelf piled high with cheese.

Peter's mouth watered. His stomach rumbled.

"What would you like to eat?" asked a lady wearing a purple robe and a long golden necklace.

“I want two of everything,” said Peter.

“Give me your coins and you can have whatever you want,” she said.

“We don’t have any coins,” said Mary.

“No coins, no food.” The lady put her nose in the air and turned to walk away.

“But we’re hungry,” said Peter.

“I don’t care,” she said.

“How do we get coins?” asked Mary.

"It's easy," she said. "You just lie, cheat, and steal like all the other kids."

"But that's wrong," said Mary.

"That's not what the Dark Ruler told us." The lady in purple pointed to the tall pyramid building. Steps led up the side to the top, where a large statue of a snake wrapped around a throne. "The Dark Ruler said we can do anything we want."

Peter shook his head. "We can't do those things."

"Well, I guess you'll be hungry then." She pulled some coins out of a pouch around her waist and started to count.

Peter lifted his chin. "I'm not worried. God will help us."

The lady stopped counting and leaned close to Peter. "Did you say *God*?"

"Yes," said Peter.

"Let me give you a little warning." The lady looked around and then whispered, "Never, ever say the word *God* around here."

"Why not?" whispered Peter.

"The Dark Ruler only has one rule." She held up a finger. "You are not allowed to talk about God . . . or else."

Mary scooted closer. "Or else what?"

"Or else you will be locked in the dungeon beneath the Temple of the Snake." She pointed to the pyramid again. "Now leave—before we all get in trouble."

"*Grrrr!*"

"Stop it, Hank," said Peter.

Mary gasped. "That's not Hank!"

Peter turned around and saw the snarling fangs of a wolf.

4

THE TROUBLEMAKERS

"*Grrrr!*" Hank growled at the wolf.

"*Grrrr!*" The wolf growled at Hank.

The grey wolf was bigger than Hank, but Hank didn't back down.

A boy tugged a long chain around the wolf's neck. "Sit, Shadow!" The wolf sat, but he still growled through his sharp fangs.

Peter grabbed Hank's collar. "Stay back, Hank!"

"Well, well, what do we have here?" said the boy. He walked around them. "It looks like we have strangers."

Another boy joined them. Peter gulped. He was much bigger than Peter.

"Yeah, strangers," the boy grunted.

"Be quiet, Darfus!" said the first boy. "I wasn't asking you."

"Yes, Jakar," mumbled Darfus. "Sorry, Jakar."

"Now where was I, before I was so rudely interrupted?" Jakar pushed Darfus aside.

"Strangers," mumbled Darfus.

"Yes, strangers," said Jakar. "And we don't like strangers."

"We're just trying to find some food," said Peter.

"I don't care!" Jakar picked up a banana from a table, peeled it, and took a big bite.

Mary put her hands on her hips like she always did when she was getting ready to boss somebody around. "You just stole that!"

"So what?" said Jakar. "I can do whatever I

want." He picked up an apple from a basket and threw it to Shadow. The wolf swallowed it in one bite.

"Who are you?" demanded Jakar.

"My name is Peter, and this is my sister, Mary," said Peter. He tried to sound brave.

"Why are you wearing those funny clothes?" said Jakar. Darfus pointed at their clothes and laughed.

Peter felt his face turning red. "It's what we wear where we are from."

"Where's that?" Jakar's voice was getting louder and more impatient.

"We came from the fut—"

Mary kicked Peter before he could finish saying "future." Peter rubbed his shin. Mary's karate lessons were really working.

"We came from far away," said Mary. She turned and gave Peter *the look*.

"Where, exactly?" said Jakar.

"We can't tell you," said Mary.

Jakar pointed a finger in her face. "You better tell me."

Hank ran between them with his teeth showing.

Jakar let out a loud laugh. "You think your tiny wolf can protect you?"

Shadow ran up to Hank and growled.

Hank stood his ground and growled back.

"Hank is a lot tougher than you think," said Peter. "And he is much smarter than your wolf."

"Really?" said Jakar. "Then maybe I will take him."

"No, you can't have him!" shouted Peter.

Jakar pointed at Hank. "Get him!"

Darfus yanked a net out of his bag and threw it over Hank. He pulled it tight, so Hank couldn't get away.

"Now, give me that leather bag," said Jakar with a wicked smile.

"No!" Peter unzipped the bag. His hands shook as he pulled out the hatchet.

Jakar laughed. "What are you going to do with that little thing?"

Peter ran to Hank and swung the hatchet down to the ground. He chopped three times and cut open the net.

"Run!" he shouted.

Hank took off like a lightning bolt.

Jakar let go of Shadow's chain. "Get him!"

Hank charged into the food shop with Shadow on his tail. He darted under a table

and between some pots full of flowers. Shadow knocked over the table and the pots. Flowers flew everywhere.

"My flowers!" cried the lady in purple.

Hank headed toward one of the wooden posts that was holding up the roof of the food shop. Shadow was right behind him. Hank ran in circles around the post. Shadow chased him around and around. Shadow's chain wrapped tighter and tighter around the post. *Clank!* The chain pulled tight and yanked Shadow back.

"Hank, run for the woods!" shouted Peter.

Shadow growled and tugged, but he couldn't get free.

Peter grinned. "I told you Hank was smart." He put the hatchet back in the bag.

"Darfus, get the bag while I unwrap the chain." Jakar ran to Shadow.

"No problem!" Darfus smiled. He walked toward Peter and reached for the bag.

Peter gave Mary a thumbs-up. She ran straight at Darfus. She jumped in the air and aimed a spinning kick at his belly.

Darfus fell back and rolled across the dusty ground.

Peter picked up the bag. "Let's get out of here!"

He and Mary ran toward the gate. Peter took one last look backwards. He gasped. Shadow was loose.

"Hurry, Mary!"

Peter grabbed Mary's hand and dashed through the crowd. Shadow, Jakar, and Darfus were close behind. Peter could almost smell their breath—especially Shadow's.

Suddenly, a strong wind blew through the city. Dust filled the air and everyone covered their eyes.

"There's the gate!" Mary was breathing hard.

Peter pulled her through the gate. The wind blew harder.

"There they are!" shouted Jakar.

Peter turned to look. Jakar was still inside the wall.

"Get them!" Jakar said. Shadow and Darfus ran toward the gate. Another huge gust of wind blew. The gate slammed shut.

"You can run, but you can't hide!" Jakar shouted. "We'll find you."

Peter and Mary kept running until they were out of sight. Mary wiped the dust from her eyes and said, "That was close."

"Good karate kick back there," said Peter.

Mary winked at him. "Good idea to use the hatchet."

"*Woof!*" barked Hank.

Peter looked up the hill and saw Hank standing at the edge of the woods. Someone was with him.

"Who's that?" asked Mary.

Peter wiped his face with his sleeve. "I can't tell with this dust in my eyes. Let's find out."

5

Into the Woods

Peter led the way up the hill toward Hank. He wondered who was with him. He hoped it wasn't one of the mean people from the city.

"I'm tired and thirsty," said Mary. She stopped and sat down on the grassy hillside.

Peter squinted toward the hill. "It's Michael!"

The angel spread his mighty wings and flew down to meet them.

"It's so good to see you." Mary put her hands on her hips. Peter knew what was coming. "But where have you been?"

"We were in big trouble down there," Peter said, "and you didn't even help!"

"I did help," said Michael. "Who do you think slammed the gate shut?"

Peter's face got red, and he looked down. "Oh," he said. "Thanks."

"God also helped you," said Michael.

"How?" asked Mary.

Michael pointed into the air. "Where do you think all the wind came from?"

"I didn't really think about it," said Mary. "I thought we were alone."

"Remember, God is always with you," said Michael.

"I'll try," said Mary. At least Peter wasn't the only one who was embarrassed.

Michael looked around and narrowed his eyes. "Let's go into the woods. It's not safe out here."

They joined Hank at the edge of the woods.

"Let's find a safe place to talk," said Michael.

Hank barked and ran ahead.

"Wait!" Peter chased him into the woods. The dog wove in and out of the trees so fast Peter couldn't catch him. He didn't stop when Peter called him.

"*Woof, woof!*"

Peter ran in the direction of the barks. He found Hank next to a river, wagging his tail. "Good boy, Hank!"

Peter took the canteen out of the bag and filled it with the fresh, clean water. He gulped it down. Mary and Michael arrived just as he was refilling it.

"Water!" shouted Mary. She grabbed the canteen and took a big gulp.

"This looks like a good place to stop," said Michael.

Peter and Mary sat down on a fallen tree and passed the canteen back and forth.

"Now, let's go over the rules of your adventure." Michael held up one finger. "First rule: You have to solve the secret of the scroll in seven days or you will be stuck here."

Peter took the scroll out of the bag. "We definitely don't want that."

Mary crossed her arms. "This place is so bad."

Michael reached under his wings and pulled out a long sword as bright as the sun. "The world has become a very dangerous place."

Peter wished he had a sword like that. Jakar wouldn't bother them anymore.

"Where are we?" asked Mary.

"You will find out soon," said Michael.

"What's the next rule?" asked Mary.

Michael held up two fingers. "Second rule: you can't tell anyone where you are from or that you are from the future."

"Peter almost told some kids in the city," said Mary.

"But I didn't." Peter gritted his teeth. Why did she always tell on him?

Mary took another drink. "Any more rules?"

Michael held up three fingers. "Third rule: you can't try to change the past. Now, let's look at the scroll."

Peter unrolled it, revealing its strange symbols and letters. He turned it upside down and sideways. "I can't read it."

Mary grabbed it. "Let me try." She stared for a while. "It looks like it has six words."

"That's right," said Michael. "Six words that are written in Hebrew. You have seven days to solve it."

Peter noticed the sky getting dark. The sun setting behind the trees made them look spooky.

"Make that six days," said Michael.

Peter said, "But there's twice as many words as the last scroll!"

"Yes, you're right," said Michael. "Now, it's getting dark, and I must go and find the enemy—Satan. He is causing much trouble." Michael spread his mighty wings.

"Wait," said Mary. "Shouldn't you stay and protect us?"

"Remember, God is always with you." Michael flapped his wings and shot into the air like a lightning bolt.

"*Ruff!*" barked Hank.

Mary twirled her hair around her fingers.

Peter could tell she was scared. "What do we do now?" she said.

"I guess we sleep here," said Peter.

Mary shivered. "But it's getting so cold and dark."

Peter pulled everything out of the bag. "We can use the things Great-Uncle Solomon packed to build a camp."

"Good idea," said Mary.

Peter grinned. "Two good ideas in one day."

"I think that's your new record." Mary seemed to be cheering up again.

Peter pulled out the pop-up tent. He set it on the ground and grabbed the rope. "Stand back!"

Pop. Boing. Whoosh. The tent popped up and they climbed in. It was the perfect size for two kids and a dog.

"What if Jakar and Shadow try to find us tonight?" Peter's stomach rumbled. He wasn't

sure if he was hungry or nervous.

"We can't worry about it. Remember, God will take care of us," said Mary.

Just then a glow came from inside the leather bag.

"The scroll!" Peter pulled it out and unrolled it. The second word of the secret message sparkled and transformed into the word GOD. "We solved our first word!"

Mary tossed her head. "Don't you mean I solved it?"

"You might have solved the first word," said Peter. "But we still have five to go."

Mary rolled over on her side, and Hank curled up near the entrance of the tent. Peter took out the flashlight and turned it on.

"What are you doing?" said Mary. "I am trying to sleep."

Peter took out Great-Uncle Solomon's adventure journal. "I want to write something down."

Day 1

This place is dangerous. All of the people are so mean. I wonder what is inside the Temple of the Snake. I built a tent and I hope it doesn't fall on us. I also hope Jakar and Shadow don't find us.

Crack!

Mary moved closer to Peter. "What was that noise?"

"*Grrrr,*" growled Hank.

Peter grabbed Hank. "*Shhhh!*"

"Turn off the flashlight," whispered Mary.

6

Paw Prints Everywhere

The tent was dark. Peter, Mary, and Hank didn't make a sound.

Crack!

"There it is again," whispered Peter.

"Shhhh."

"What if it's Jakar and Shadow?" whispered Peter.

"Be quiet, or they might find us," Mary whispered back.

Snap! Squish! Thump! The sounds got louder outside the tent.

"If it's Jakar," said Peter, "I think he brought an army with him."

Thud! The ground rumbled and shook.

Mary's eyes opened wide. "Something *huge* is coming."

"Maybe it's Darfus," said Peter.

"No," said Mary. "Bigger!"

"Bigger than Darfus?" said Peter.

Thud! Thud!

"Yes," said Mary. "Much bigger."

Then everything was completely quiet.

"What was it?" said Peter.

"I don't know," said Mary. "But I hope it doesn't come back."

Peter was surprised that Mary and Hank could fall asleep. Hank was even snoring. Peter lay awake for a long time, listening for any noises. He was sure he would never fall asleep.

The next thing Peter knew, light was shining

on his face. He sat up and rubbed his eyes. The light was streaming through the crack in the tent flap.

Mary yawned and stretched. "Is it already morning?"

"Yes. Let's go see what happened last night," said Peter.

"Do you think it's safe?" said Mary.

Peter slowly poked his head out of the tent. "I think so. I don't see anything scary."

Hank ran out and sniffed all around. "*Woof! Woof!*"

Peter grabbed the leather bag and ran over to see what Hank had found. "Look at all the paw prints. There must be thousands!"

Mary came up behind him. "These are from a bear." She looked to the right. "It looks like there were two bears."

Peter ran to the other side of the tent. "Look

at these prints. They're huge!"

Mary put her hand inside one of them. "This is from an elephant. Those prints are from a horse," she said, pointing. "And those are from a camel."

"How do you know so much about paw prints?" asked Peter.

"I read a book called *Know Your Paws: A Complete Guide to the Animal Kingdom*."

"Your reading is paying off," said Peter.

"I want to be ready for anything," said Mary.

Peter looked ahead. "It looks like the prints go that way."

Mary took out the compass. "They're going west."

Peter quickly packed everything back into the bag. "Let's go!" he said.

They followed the trail of prints and came to an open field covered with tree trunks.

"Who cut down all these trees?" asked Mary.

"I think I know." Peter pointed to the top of a hill. "That's one huge boat!"

"Woof, woof!"

Peter turned around to see what Hank was barking at.

Two tall giraffes came out of the woods. They walked past Peter and headed up the hill toward the huge wooden boat.

Thud! Thud! Two rhinos crashed through the woods.

Squeak, squeak. Two mice ran between Mary's feet.

"*Eek!*" Mary screamed and ran behind a tree.

Peter shook his head. “I can’t believe you’re afraid of mice, but not rhinos.”

Mary slowly came from behind the tree.

Hank barked at the animals and made sure they stayed on the trail. Peter was proud. After all, Hank was a herding dog. Peter had just never seen him in action before.

“Look at the poor little turtles,” said Mary. The little shelled guys were falling behind the other animals.

“I don’t think they will ever make it,” said Peter. He picked them up.

Just then, the bag glowed. Peter unzipped it and unrolled the scroll. The fourth word glowed and transformed into WILL.

“I solved one!” Peter did a happy dance.

"Two down," said Mary, "and four to go."

"Woof, woof!"

Peter looked up and saw a man with a long brown beard walking down the hill. He looked about the same age as their dad.

"Who do we have here?" said the man.

Peter quickly rolled up the scroll and hid it in the bag. "My name is Peter."

"And I'm Mary." She didn't seem worried at all. It was almost like she knew who he was.

"Ruff!"

"And this is Hank," said Peter.

"My name is Shem," said the man.

Mary leaned over and whispered in Peter's ear, "I knew it was him."

"How?" Peter whispered back.

"Maybe you should read your Bible."

Shem pointed at all the animals walking up the hill. "Did you bring all of these?"

"No," said Mary. "We're hiding from Jakar and Shadow."

Shem's face darkened as he nodded. "I understand. You can stay with us. We'll keep you safe."

"Follow me," said Shem.

"Thanks," said Mary.

They walked toward the big boat. Animals were everywhere.

"They all started showing up last night," Shem said.

"We heard," said Peter.

"Where are you from?" asked Shem.

"We are from the fut—"

Mary kicked Peter in the shin. Again.

Peter rubbed his leg.

Mary gave Peter another look. Peter was surprised her face didn't get stuck that way. "We are from far, far away."

"Well, welcome to the ark!" said Shem.

"It's one huge boat!" said Peter.

"Don't call it a boat in front of my dad," said Shem. "He wants everyone to call it the ARK."

"Okay," said Peter. "It's one huge ark!"

They arrived at the top of the hill. Peter was out of breath and ready to eat.

"It looks even bigger up here!" Mary said.

Peter ran beside the ark. "It's almost two football fields long."

Shem tilted his head. "What's football?"

"It's a game where we come from," said Peter.

"You'll have to teach me," said Shem. "It gets boring up here building the ark."

"How long have you been working on it?" asked Mary.

Shem counted his fingers—several times. "About a hundred years."

Peter's jaw dropped. "You don't look a hundred years old."

"Thanks," said Shem. "If you think I'm old, wait until you meet my parents."

"How old are they?" asked Mary.

"Six hundred," said Shem. "But they're in great shape. I'm sure they're around here somewhere." He looked around and shrugged.

"Do you want a tour of the ark?" said Shem.

"Sure!" said Peter. He hoped food would be involved.

7

The Ark

"How do we get in?" asked Mary.

"There's only one door," said Shem. "It's on the other side."

Animals were sleeping all around the ark. Peter tiptoed quietly between two snoring alligators. Two pink flamingos each stood on one leg and slept. One of the tigers was awake and purred as Mary walked past. Hank chased the sheep and cows around in circles.

"I've never seen many of these animals," said Shem. "They must have come from far away."

"Mary knows a lot about animals," said Peter. "Ask her if you have any questions."

They finally made it to the other side.

Shem pointed to a long ramp leading to a door in the side. "Are you ready to go in?"

Peter ran up the ramp. He could hear Mary and Hank racing up after him.

"Wait for me," said Shem.

But Peter couldn't wait. He ran through the door and stopped. "It's bigger than I ever imagined." He walked to the center of the ark and stared up. Large wooden beams went from the bottom to the top. Peter could barely see the roof of the ark, it was so high.

The sun shone through a row of windows at the top. Peter walked up the ramp leading to each floor from the center of the ark. He couldn't believe how many cages there were. "There must be thousands of them," he said.

Shem joined Peter on the ramp. "We've been busy for the last hundred years."

Mary joined them. "Where are all the animals?"

"Outside," said Shem. "We need to make sure everything's ready before we let them in."

Peter sniffed the air. "What's that smell?"

"Are you hungry?" said Shem.

Peter nodded so hard he thought his head might fall off.

"We haven't eaten in two days," Mary said.

"*Ruff!*" barked Hank.

"Why didn't you tell me?" said Shem. "We have lots of food. Follow me."

They walked up the ramp to the third floor. A delicious smell floated out of the kitchen. Peter followed his nose to a brick oven.

"Look at all this food!" Peter looked at the shelves filled with fruits, vegetables, corn, berries, bread, and potatoes—lots of potatoes. Behind the shelves were piles of wheat and sacks of flour and grain. More fruits and vegetables grew in large pots. Shem walked to the table where a big round guy was slurping soup from a bowl. "This is my brother Ham. He's always eating."

"Nice to meet you," said Peter.

Ham looked up. "Nice to meet you."

"These children need to eat," said a short lady wearing an apron. She brought two bowls of soup and some bread and set it on the table.

"This is my wife," said Ham.

"*Woof!*" barked Hank.

Ham's wife set a bowl of food on the ground. "We can't forget you."

Peter wasn't sure how many bowls Mary and Hank ate, but he had three.

"Where's Japheth?" asked Shem.

Ham took another bite of bread. "Probably working. He's always working."

Shem took Peter, Mary, and Hank down to the second floor.

Clank! Clank! Japheth was hammering a hinge onto the door of a cage. "Finished!" He swung it shut. "This should be the last one!"

Peter looked around the shop. "You have a lot of nice tools." He picked up a hammer and a saw.

"Thanks," said

Japheth. "I've built many cages over the years."

"Shem! Ham! Japheth!" a woman's voice echoed though the ark. "Where are you?" A lady walked in and said, "There you are."

"This is our mom," said Shem.

"You don't look six hundred years old," said Peter.

Shem's mom smiled at Peter. "Well, thank you very much."

"They came with the animals," said Shem.

"We have come to help," said Mary.

"We can use it." Shem's mom turned to her sons. "Your dad wants to have a family meeting. He said God has given him a very important message."

They walked all the way up the ramp to the very top deck. Peter squeezed through a small opening onto the top of the ark. He could hear Mary grunting behind him.

A tall man with a long white beard and a blue robe stood at the far edge. "Welcome," he said. "My name is Noah."

Peter nodded, but he couldn't say a word. He might not have read the Bible as much as Mary, but he knew who Noah was.

"I understand you are here to help," said Noah.

"Yes," said Mary.

"We can use it," said Noah. "Time is running out!"

"What do you mean?" said Shem.

Noah walked to the edge of the ark and looked into the distance. "The flood is coming!"

8

GET READY!

"When is the flood coming?" asked Ham.

"Soon," Noah said. "Very soon!"

"Are we ready?" asked Shem.

Two eagles flew over Peter's head. Doves landed near his feet. Birds covered the top deck.

"I don't know if *we're* ready," said Noah. "But God is."

"I finished the last cage," Japheth said.

Noah walked to the edge of the ark. "It was about a hundred years ago when God told me to build this ark because He is sending a flood."

"Why?" asked Mary.

Noah looked down at the woods. "It broke God's heart to see what has happened to his amazing creation."

"What's happened?" said Peter.

Noah shook his head. "Things have gone wrong. Darkness and evil have covered the earth."

"What do you mean?" asked Mary.

Noah pointed toward the city. "The earth is full of violence, sickness, hate, and greed. It is not what God created it to be."

Peter remembered how beautiful the Garden of Eden used to be. "It was perfect."

"The world has gotten so bad that God is sending a flood to wash it clean," said Noah. "To start over."

He sat on the deck. "God will use the ark to rescue the animals and the people who believe."

An owl landed on Noah's shoulder. "Everyone else will be destroyed by the flood."

"*Whooooo!*" hooted the owl.

"Everyone," said Noah. "But God promised to rescue me and my family. We are the only people left who have faith in God."

"What about the other good people in the world?" asked Peter.

"There are none." Noah pointed at the Temple of the Snake. "They have all turned against God."

Mary thought for a moment. "Maybe if you told them about the flood, they would believe and follow God."

Noah shook his head. "I have been telling them for more than a hundred years."

"What do they say?" asked Peter.

"They laugh and make fun of me." Noah petted Hank's head. "They don't trust God. They would rather do what they want."

"That's sad," said Mary.

Noah's wife hugged him. "Yes, it is."

"There were times I wondered if I was crazy," said Noah. "I had to learn to always trust God."

Peter looked over the side of the ark. "Look, more animals are coming!"

"I hope we have enough cages," said Japheth.

Ham rubbed his belly. "I hope we have enough food!"

"Dad," said Shem. "Mom said God gave you an important message."

"Oh, yes," said Noah. "God told me the flood is coming soon."

"When?" asked Shem.

"In seven days," said Noah.

"Seven days to get ready?" Shem said.

Peter watched a shadow fall across his shoe. He looked up and saw the sun setting behind the trees.

Noah looked too and counted on his fingers. "Actually we only have five days left."

Ham dropped the loaf of bread he was eating. "Five days!"

"Yes," said Noah. "So get some sleep. We have a lot of work to do."

"Where do we sleep?" asked Peter.

"Follow me," said Shem's wife.

She led them to a room on the third floor.

"This is nice," said Peter, plopping on a soft bag full of fluffy wool.

“Just make yourselves at home. We will wake you in the morning.” She walked out and shut the door.

“What an amazing day,” said Mary. “Can you believe we are actually on the ark?”

“I can’t believe it,” said Peter. “I want to write something in the journal so I don’t forget.”

Peter crawled into the fluffy bed. He propped the journal on his knees and wrote.

Day 2

The ark is much bigger than I imagined—about as long as two football fields. I saw thousands of animals and more keep coming. I'm not sure what some of them are. Noah and his family are the only nice people we have met. They are taking care of us. We have lots of work to do before the flood comes.

Peter closed the journal and fell asleep with Hank curled up beside him.

9

All Aboard!

The next morning, Noah woke Peter and Mary for a breakfast meeting. Noah's wife told them to get something to eat before Ham ate it all.

Peter didn't have to be told twice. He dug into the eggs.

"We need a plan to get the animals on the ark," Noah said.

"Ask Mary," said Peter, with his mouth full. "She knows everything about animals."

"What do you think, Mary?" said Shem. "Where should we put all the animals?"

Mary unrolled one of Noah's blank scrolls. She drew an ark with lines across it for the three floors. She wrote the word *Big* on the bottom floor. "The bottom floor is tall and has bigger cages."

She drew a bear on the bottom floor. "If an animal is bigger than a bear, bring it to the bottom floor. It will be a good place for animals like elephants, hippos, rhinos, horses, bears, and buffalo."

"What about the middle floor?" asked Shem.

Mary wrote the word *Medium* on the scroll. "Move the medium-sized animals to the middle floor. It's a good place for animals like sheep, pigs, deer, wolves, lions, tigers, alligators, and kangaroos. Just don't put the wolves and sheep next to each other."

"Should we put the monkeys in the middle?" said Peter. He laughed. No one else did.

Mary looked at Peter without blinking. "You

get the idea." She drew a monkey on the middle floor.

Ham took a bite of a banana. "What about the top floor?"

Mary wrote the word *Small* on the scroll. "Take the tiny animals to the top floor. It's perfect for turtles, rabbits, raccoons, bats, bugs, butterflies, and birds . . . lots of birds."

Noah stood up. "We have a plan!"

"We all work together," said Shem.

"Yes," said Mary. "Teamwork makes the dream work."

"That's what my mom always says," Peter said. He was really starting to miss his parents.

Everyone headed off the ark to start bringing in the big animals.

Hank barked at them and chased them into the cages. After all, he was a herding dog.

Peter hopped on the back of a horse and joined Hank. They chased the cow and bull into a cage. Mary shut the cage door.

"*Yeehaw!* I'm a cowboy!" shouted Peter.

"What's a cowboy?" said Shem.

"It's a guy who rides a horse," said Peter.

"Why don't you call them *horseboys*?" asked Shem.

Peter shrugged. "I don't know."

Once all the big animals were in, they began to bring in the medium animals.

"Everybody stand back!" shouted Mary. "Here come the alligators."

Peter shut them in their cage. "They don't look like they're in a good mood this morning."

The lions and tigers went into their cages. Peter slammed the doors quickly. He couldn't believe he was this close to wild animals.

"Help with these monkeys!" shouted Ham. "I can't reach them."

The monkeys had climbed up the wooden beams and were swinging from the roof.

Peter ran down to the bottom floor and got one of the giraffes. Back on the monkey deck, he climbed up the giraffe's tall neck. But he still couldn't reach them.

"I have an idea," said Mary. She ran to the kitchen and came back with a bunch of bananas. She held them in the air. The monkeys swung down. She tossed the bananas in their cage, and the monkeys followed.

When the middle floor was full, the group

ate lunch before they began to gather the small animals and birds.

Peter carried the turtles to the top floor. Hank chased the squirrels into their cage.

"Everyone duck!" shouted Peter, as the birds flew through the top windows. Colorful feathers were everywhere. Peter shut the last door of the last cage.

"We did it!" shouted Noah. "All the animals and birds are in the ark."

Peter tried to give Noah a high five. But Noah just looked at Peter's hand. "That was awkward," mumbled Peter.

After a big dinner, everyone headed off to their bedrooms.

Peter took out

Great-Uncle Solomon's journal and wrote about his exciting day.

Day 3

Hank is great at herding the animals. I hope we have enough food. My back is sore from riding the horse. Mary sneezed all day. I am not sure if she more allergic to hay or to work. And those monkeys are going to drive me crazy!

Ding! Ding! Peter tossed the journal in the bag and scrambled to the door. Noah was running down the hall ringing a bell.

"We have an emergency!" said Noah. "The monkeys escaped and are letting out the other animals."

They ran to the middle deck, where monkeys were swinging through the ark. Animals were everywhere.

Peter pushed the sheep back into their cage. Ham pulled the pigs into theirs. Mary used a net to catch birds. Japheth grabbed the turtles—they hadn't gotten very far. Finally, Noah's wife found some more bananas and tricked the monkeys again.

Peter, Mary, and Hank made one last round to make sure all the animals were in their cages and the doors were shut tight.

Peter stopped at the tiger's cage and stared. There was only one tiger inside. There were supposed to be two of everything. "I think we have a problem!" he shouted.

Mary and Hank were there in a flash.

"What's wrong?" Mary said.

Peter pointed at the half-empty cage.

Growl!

Peter whirled around.

The missing tiger was crouched low, and he was creeping right toward them.

10

A Big Problem

Hank growled at the tiger, but the tiger snarled and crept forward.

Roar!

Peter turned toward the new sound. A lion was standing on top of the tiger's cage! The lion roared again, and the tiger ran back into the cage. Then the lion leapt down and walked back into his own cage.

Peter slammed the doors shut. "I see why they call you the king of the beasts."

Peter's heart was still pounding as he climbed

into bed. It seemed like just a few minutes until Peter heard *cock-a-doodle-doo* echo through the ark.

"Is it already time to get up?" asked Mary.

Peter opened the door and held his nose. "Yuck! What's that smell?"

"What do you think it is?" said Mary. "All these animals have to go to the bathroom somewhere."

Japheth walked up to Peter and handed him a shovel. "You are with me on cleanup duty."

Peter gagged. "I hope this doesn't take very long."

Japheth's wife walked toward them. "Mary, you

can come with me. We are going to collect some chicken eggs for breakfast."

Mary waved as they walked up the ramp. "Have fun!"

Peter shook his head. Why did Mary always get the easy jobs?

Japheth opened the first cage and shoveled out the mess. He walked all the way to the door of the ark and threw it out.

"This is going to take forever," said Peter. "But I have an idea."

"What?" said Japheth.

"Do you have a big box and wheels and two poles?" said Peter.

"Yes," said Japheth. "In the shop."

"Let's go!" said Peter.

Within a few minutes, Peter had made a wheelbarrow.

"What does it do?" said Japheth.

Peter put it on the floor and rolled it around. "You can shovel the mess in here. Then I can roll it to dump it outside."

Japheth seemed impressed. After that, cleanup duty didn't take long at all.

After breakfast, it was time to feed the animals. With so many animals, it took all day.

Before they went to bed that night, Noah said, "Let's sing praises to God."

Musical instruments were brought out. Shem played the horn, and his wife played the harp. Everyone sang out loud.

"Where did you get the instruments?" asked Mary.

"My brother Jubal made them," said Noah.

"I didn't know you had a brother," said Peter.

Noah's shoulders slumped. "Yes, but he died several years ago. He was one of the last people who had faith in God."

Shem's wife strummed the harp. "We remember him by playing music."

The sun went down, and Peter, Mary, and Hank went to bed. Peter wrote in the journal.

Day 4

Mary is getting all of the easy jobs. I was stuck on cage-cleaning duty. Elephants and hippos make a big mess—if you know what I mean. I think the ark is almost ready. It was fun to sing with Noah's family. I am glad they are keeping music alive.

The next morning, *cock-a-doodle-doo* echoed through the ark again.

"That rooster is getting on my nerves!" said Peter.

At breakfast, Peter asked something he'd been thinking about. "Noah, how did you know how to make the ark the perfect size for all the animals?"

"God told me," said Noah. "He said to build it 300 cubits long, 50 cubits wide, and 30 cubits tall."

"What's a cubit?" said Peter.

Mary put down her bread. "A cubit is an ancient measurement."

"Who are you calling ancient?" said Noah. "I'm only six hundred years old."

Everyone laughed.

"A cubit is about 16 inches," said Mary. "So that means the ark is about 450 feet long, 75 feet wide, and 45 feet wide."

Peter shook his head. "How do you know that?"

"I read it in a book titled *Ancient Measurement: How Do We Measure Up?*," said Mary.

Of course she did, thought Peter.

"I guess God knew what he was doing," said Peter.

"I did everything God told me," Noah said. "You can trust God."

Peter was amazed how much Noah and his family trusted God. Especially since no one else in the world did.

Peter, Mary, and Hank spent the day checking to make sure all the animals were in their cages.

"We have another big problem," said Mary. "There is only one wolf. The female."

"Why is that a big problem?" asked Peter.

"Remember the book I showed you at Great-Uncle Solomon's house?"

Peter nodded.

"All dogs come from wolves," said Mary.

Peter stared blankly.

“If we don’t have a male and female wolf,” Mary paused. She looked at Hank and continued, “there won’t be any dogs in the future.”

“We better find that wolf!” shouted Peter.

“*Ruff!*” barked Hank.

Peter searched from one end of the ark to the other. He looked behind every cage and under every table. But there was no male wolf.

Before going to sleep, Peter wrote in the journal.

Day 5

We have to find the male wolf. If we don't, there won't be any dogs in the future. That means no Hank. I am also worried that we still have four words to solve in the scroll and we only have two days left. ______ GOD ______ WILL ______ _____.

11

The Temple of the Snake

The next morning Noah called everyone out of bed and took them to the door of the ark. "Look! The elephants broke one of the hinges. If we don't fix it, the ark will sink! Someone needs to go to the city and try to find an iron hinge."

"We'll go," said Mary.

Peter's palms started to sweat. "Why can't someone else go?" He whispered to Mary.

"We have to do it," Mary whispered back. "I'll tell you why on the way."

Peter took a deep breath and agreed.

"You're very brave," said Noah. "Take this money to buy the hinge. It's all we have, but I don't think we will need money after today."

"Why?" said Peter.

"The flood is coming tomorrow," said Noah.

"We better hurry!" Peter grabbed the leather bag and they left.

"Why did we have to be the ones to get the hinge?" asked Peter as they went into the woods.

"We can't risk the Dark Ruler capturing one of Noah's family," answered Mary.

"What about us?" said Peter.

"The Bible says that Noah and all of his family were in the ark . . . not us," said Mary. "We have to make sure that happens."

Peter's stomach rumbled from nervousness. "But what if Jakar and Shadow find us?"

"We have to trust God," said Mary.

The bag shook. "Wait!" Peter unzipped it and pulled out the scroll. The first word glowed and transformed into the word TRUST. "We solved three words," he said, holding up the scroll.

TRUST GOD _____ WILL ______ ______

Peter rolled up the scroll and put it back in the bag. They walked down into the valley.

Peter stopped at the gate. "Let's find a hinge and get back to the ark."

"Where do we find one?" said Mary.

Clank! Clank!

Mary covered her ears. "What is that noise?"

Peter pointed to a large work area surrounded by a black iron fence. "It's coming from over there."

The sign above the entrance read, Tubal Cain's Blacksmith Shop.

"Maybe they have hinges," said Mary.

When Peter walked in, a man with a bushy gray beard and wide shoulders was holding a long iron rod over the fire. The man pulled it out and pounded it with a huge hammer.

"What are you are making?" asked Peter.

The man stopped pounding and looked at Peter. He held the red-hot iron in front of him and walked straight toward Peter. "If you're not going to buy anything, then leave."

Peter took a deep breath. "We do want to buy something. We have money."

The man put down his hammer and rod. "Well, why didn't you say so? How can I help you?"

"We need a large hinge," said Peter.

"For what?" said the man.

"It's for the door of the ark," said Mary.

"Is my crazy brother still building that boat?" said the man.

Peter eyebrows went up. "Noah is your brother?"

"Yes," said the man. "My name is Tubal Cain."

"I didn't know Noah had another brother," said Mary.

"We haven't spoken in years," said Tubal Cain, picking up a big piece of metal. "This hinge should work." He took out his hammer and chisel and pounded something onto the hinge. "Here you go."

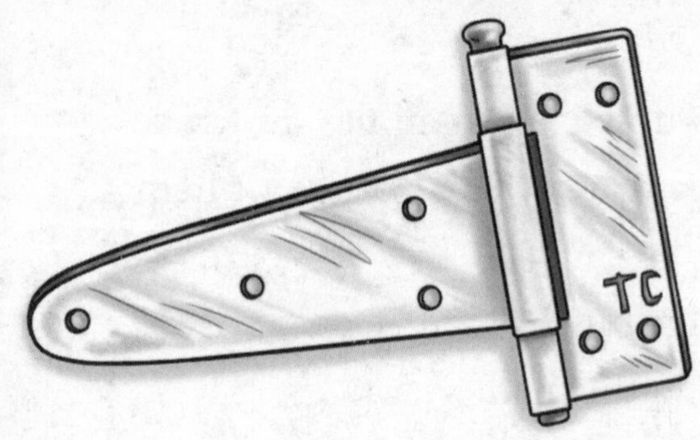

Peter turned it over. The letters TC were engraved on the hinge.

"Maybe someday crazy Noah will finish the ark," said Tubal Cain.

"Maybe sooner than you think," said Peter.

Mary tugged Peter's arm and gave the blacksmith the coins. Peter put the hinge in the bag. He was glad to get out of there. Then they walked out the door and saw Shadow standing in front of them.

He was growling and his fangs were showing. Jakar and Darfus stood right behind him. Peter's eyes bulged.

"Well, well, look who we have here!" said Jakar. "Get them!"

"Run!" shouted Peter. But before he could

take even one step, Darfus pulled a net from behind his back and threw it over Hank.

"Not this time!" said Jakar.

He yanked a rope from his waist and whipped it around Peter and Mary.

"Let us go!" Mary shouted.

Peter twisted and turned, but there was no escape.

"I think it's time you met the Dark Ruler," said Jakar. "Tie their hands, Darfus."

Darfus tied their hands tightly. Peter's heart pounded as Darfus dragged them up the steps to the Temple of the Snake. Jakar sneered and laughed at them. When they reached the top of the pyramid, Darfus untied them and pulled the net off Hank.

"We captured them!" said Jakar proudly.

The Dark Ruler was sitting on a throne surrounded by a large statue of a snake. He wore a black robe with a hood covering most of his face. He held a thorny staff with a snake slithering around it.

"Good work," said the Dark Ruler. "Here is your reward." He tossed a bag to Jakar.

Peter heard coins jingling.

"Are you into snakes?" asked Peter, with a nervous grin.

The Dark Ruler did not smile. "Jakar says you three have been causing problems in the city."

"We were just buying a hinge," said Peter.

"Why would little children need a hinge?" said the Dark Ruler.

"We need it to finish the ark," said Mary.

The Dark Ruler stood up and walked to the edge of the temple. "You mean that old fool is almost finished?"

"Noah is not a fool," said Peter. "All the animals are on board."

The Dark Ruler pointed across the woods at the ark on top of the hill. “Noah is crazy!”

“No he’s not,” said Peter. “God told him the flood is coming!”

The Dark Ruler pointed his staff in Peter’s face. “Did you say *GOD*?” The snake slithered to the top of the staff and stared into Peter’s eyes.

Peter took a step back. “Yes.”

The Dark Ruler slammed the rod down.

"There is NO GOD! He is dead!" Suddenly, a bolt of lightning cracked through the sky.

Peter gasped. "You're lying. God's alive. He's going to rescue the animals and Noah's family."

Just then the leather bag started to shake and glow.

"What's in there?" said the Dark Ruler.

Peter unzipped the bag and pulled out the scroll. The third and fifth words glowed and transformed into HE and RESCUE.

"Ahh, I thought you looked familiar," said the Dark Ruler.

"I don't think we've met," said Peter.

The Dark Ruler walked slowly around Peter. "It was a long, long time ago." The snake hissed at Peter. "I looked a little different then."

A chill ran down Peter's back. "You're Satan, the enemy."

The Dark Ruler slowly clapped his hands. "Congratulations. You figured it out."

"But it's too late," he added. "My plan is almost complete. Nearly every person has turned against God. I have just one family left."

"You won't win," said Peter.

The Dark Ruler grabbed the scroll out of Peter's hand. "Who's going to stop me?"

"God will stop you!" shouted Peter.

The Dark Ruler turned around. "Take them to the dungeon!"

12

Dark Clouds

"Make sure they don't escape!" said the Dark Ruler. "I have a family to visit."

"They won't get away this time," said Jakar. "Shadow will make sure of it!"

The sun began to set as Jakar and Darfus led Peter, Mary, and Hank to the dungeon. They walked down the stone steps and through a long, dark hallway filled with spider webs.

Darfus pushed them into a damp and smelly jail cell and slammed the gate shut.

Jakar wrapped a heavy chain around the gate

and locked it. "There," he said. "That should keep you inside!"

"Please let us out," said Mary. Her voice was shaky, like she was about to cry.

"Never," said Jakar. He emptied the bag of coins onto the ground and counted them.

Shadow growled at his prisoners.

"We'll be back in the morning," said Jakar. "Shadow, keep guard."

"But . . . you can't leave us here," said Mary. "Where are you going?"

Jakar and Darfus laughed as they walked away. "We're going to spend our reward!"

It was dark and cold in the dungeon. Peter and Mary huddled close. Then Peter pulled matches out of his pocket and lit one.

"Where did you get those?" said Mary.

"I took them out of the bag before they dragged us down here," said Peter.

Mary looked around. Her eyes looked big and scared. "Where is the bag?"

"It's still at the top of the pyramid," said Peter. "And so is the scroll."

"What are we going to do?" said Mary.

"I don't know," said Peter.

Every so often, Shadow would stop and growl through the gate. Hank growled back. They walked back and forth at the gate. Then they stopped growling and looked into each other's eyes.

Peter lit another match. "It's like they know each other."

Peter looked again. Shadow was wagging his tail! The big, bad wolf was wagging his tail.

Peter wanted to laugh. "Maybe Shadow is Hank's great-great-great-great-great-grandfather."

Mary snapped her fingers. "That's it!"

"*What's* it?" said Peter.

"What if Shadow *is* Hank's great-great-great-great-great-grandfather?" said Mary.

Peter scratched his head. "He doesn't look that old."

"Don't you get it?" said Mary. "Shadow is the male wolf that is supposed to be on the ark."

"Of course!" said Peter. "So there can be dogs in the future."

Mary shook the chains on the door. "We have to figure out how to get out of here. If only Michael were here."

Just then, a gust of wind blew through the dungeon. It blew out Peter's match. It was completely dark.

Whoosh!

"Who's there?" he shouted.

A shape moved closer. Shadow ran to the corner. Suddenly, a large blazing sword flashed through the air and through the chains. They shattered and fell to the ground. The jail cell gate swung wide open.

Peter lit another match and held it up. "Michael!"

"Who did you think it was?" said Michael.

"Where have you been?" asked Mary.

Michael put his sword away. "I have been trying to find Satan."

"We found him," said Peter. "He's the Dark Ruler."

"We have to get to the ark!" said Mary.

"First we have to get the hinge," said Peter.

"Where is it?" said Michael.

Peter's shoulders sagged. "At the top of the temple."

"We must go and find it!" said Michael.

They climbed the stone steps to the top of the Temple of the Snake. Shadow followed close behind. Hank sniffed around and found the bag beside the throne. The Dark Ruler was gone, and so was the scroll.

"We better get back to the ark and warn Noah!" said Peter.

Shadow joined them in their escape back to the ark. Michael led them through the dark woods, lighting the way with his blazing sword.

"I must find Satan. He can't destroy the ark!" Michael spread his mighty wings and flew into the sky.

As Peter, Mary, Hank, and Shadow began the long climb to the top of the hill, the sun began to rise.

Noah ran down to meet them. "You made

it!" he shouted. "And you found the male wolf. But what took you so long?"

Peter pulled the hinge out of the bag. "It's a long story."

Noah looked up as dark clouds filled the sky. "We don't have much time!"

They ran up the hill and climbed the long ramp to the ark door. Japheth was waiting for them with a large hammer and nails. He quickly repaired the door.

"Now we are ready," said Noah. "Everyone in the ark!"

Peter went with Noah as they led Shadow to his cage and took one last look through the ark to make sure the family and animals were in place.

"Oh no!" said Noah. "We're missing another animal!"

"Hank can find it," said Peter. "Come on, Hank."

"I don't think Hank is big enough to handle this animal," said Noah.

"Which one is missing?" asked Mary.

"The lion," answered Noah.

13

The Rainbow

Peter headed into the woods with Mary and Hank. More dark clouds filled the sky.

Peter stopped. “What if we don’t find him?”

“What if we don’t find *the scroll*?” asked Mary.

“I almost forgot about that,” said Peter.

“How could you forget about the scroll?” said Mary. “If we don’t solve it today, we will be stuck here forever!”

Lightning struck. Thunder rolled.

Hank barked and ran to the edge of the woods.

Peter followed. "Did you find the lion?"

"Not exactly!" said an evil voice.

Peter stopped in his tracks and stared up at the Dark Ruler. Peter's heart pounded in his chest.

The Dark Ruler pulled the scroll out of a velvet bag. "Are you looking for this?"

"Give it back!" shouted Peter.

"Your scroll might have amazing power, but I can't figure out how to use it. I will give it back if you join me," said the Dark Ruler. His cold, dark eyes squinted. "Then we will destroy the ark and we can rule the world."

"We will never join you!" shouted Peter.

"Then I will destroy you and the scroll!" shouted the Dark Ruler.

Roar! The lion crashed through the trees and stood face to face with the Dark Ruler.

"No!" cried the Dark Ruler.

Roar! The lion leapt at him.

"You will not stop my plan!" The Dark Ruler dropped the scroll and swung his staff at the lion. It sent the lion rolling.

The lion shook his golden mane and stood up on his massive paws.

A bolt of light sliced through the sky. It hit the Dark Ruler and knocked him back into the woods. Then the bolt of light transformed into Michael.

He drew his blazing sword.

"I thought I might see you," said the Dark Ruler.

"You will not win!" shouted Michael.

"Who is going to stop me?"

"We are!" Michael spread his mighty wings and flew straight at the Dark Ruler.

The lion leapt and joined Michael.

Sparks flew from Michael's sword. Branches snapped under the lion's powerful claws. It was a blur of fur and light and darkness.

"*Woof! Woof!*"

"No, Hank!" said Peter. "Stay here."

"Hurry!" said Mary. "Get the scroll!"

Peter picked up the scroll. Then he turned and headed toward the ark, with Mary and Hank close behind.

As they ran up the hill again to meet Noah, Peter heard roars and hisses echoing through the woods. Then it was completely quiet.

Peter looked up as thunder rumbled in the sky. A jagged fork of lightning lit up the darkness, and rain began to fall.

"Quick! On the ark! Come with us," said Noah, standing at the top of the ramp.

"We can't," said Mary.

"But you will drown," said Noah.

"God will help us," said Peter.

God started to shut the door of the ark.

"Wait! The lion!" shouted Peter. The huge door continued to shut.

Roar! The lion bolted out of the woods. He made a mighty leap into the ark as the door was closing.

The rain fell more quickly, and water rushed from cracks in the ground.

"What are we going to do?" said Mary.

"We have to solve the scroll," said Peter. "Or we will drown."

Peter looked down the hill toward the city. Water crashed through the city walls. It rose and covered the Temple of the Snake.

"We have to hurry!" said Peter. "The flood is coming!" He unrolled the scroll.

"We need the last word," Mary said, her voice shaking.

"Trust God He Will Rescue Noah," said Peter.

Nothing happened to the scroll.

"Trust God He Will Rescue Animals," said Mary.

Nothing happened.

The water reached Peter and Mary's knees. It rose above their shoulders. Hank paddled in the water. Peter and Mary struggled to stay afloat. The rain pounded harder.

Peter knew he couldn't stay afloat much longer. He threw the scroll to Mary. "Maybe you can solve it, and God will rescue you."

He took one more deep breath before he was pulled under the water. He saw Mary's legs kicking and Hank paddling.

Then Peter saw something glowing above the water. He struggled to the top one more time.

Mary was holding the scroll above the water.

Peter had solved the last word: TRUST GOD. HE WILL RESCUE YOU.

The water whirled in a circle away from them.

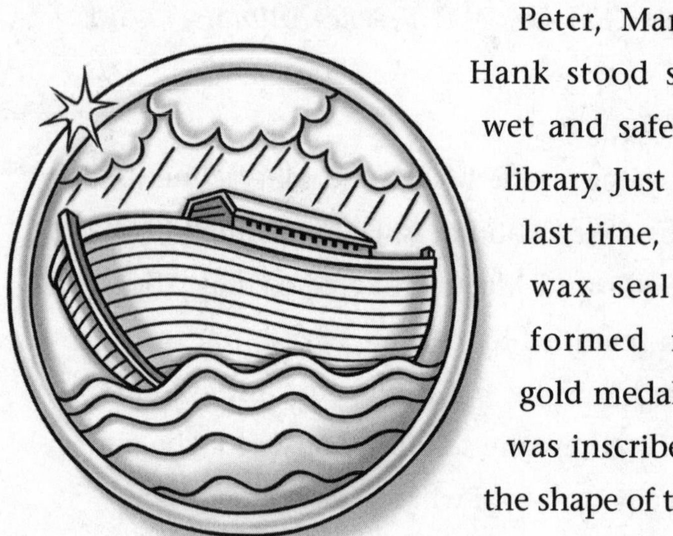

Peter, Mary, and Hank stood soaking wet and safe in the library. Just like the last time, the red wax seal transformed into a gold medallion. It was inscribed with the shape of the ark.

Great-Uncle Solomon raced into the library. "What happened?"

Peter told Great-Uncle Solomon about their amazing adventure. He told him about all the animals and how huge the ark was. Mary told him about the Temple of the Snake and the Dark Ruler.

Hank shook and water flew everywhere.

Great-Uncle Solomon wiped his glasses with his shirt. "That is an amazing adventure!"

Peter pulled the journal out of the leather bag. "I wrote all about it in your journal."

"I just hope Noah and his family were okay," said Mary.

Great-Uncle Solomon went to one of the shelves in the library and grabbed his big red Bible. "Let me tell you the rest of the story," he said.

He told them it rained for forty days and forty nights. Then Great-Uncle Solomon told them that the ark landed on the top of Mount Ararat. But Noah and his family and the animals had to wait a whole year before the water dried up and they could get off the ark.

"They were in the ark for a whole year?" asked Mary.

"Yes," said Great-Uncle Solomon.

"I'm glad we packed so much food in there," said Peter.

"Yes," said Great-Uncle Solomon. "God made sure they had everything they needed."

He turned the page of his Bible. He told them that Noah's family and the animals got safely off the ark. And God made a rainbow in the sky as a promise to never destroy the earth with the flood again.

"It was like a new beginning for God's creation," said Great-Uncle Solomon.

"What happened to the ark?" asked Mary.

"Years ago, I went on an archaeological dig on Mount Ararat in search of it," he said.

"Did you find it?" said Mary.

"No, I only found one thing."

"What?" said Mary.

"Wait here," said Great-Uncle Solomon. He came back with something wrapped in a red cloth.

When he unwrapped it, Peter gasped. Great-Uncle Solomon was holding a rusty hinge.

"Can I see it?" asked Peter. He turned the hinge over and rubbed some dirt off the back. The initials TC were engraved there.

"This is the hinge we bought from Tubal Cain for the ark door!" Peter said.

Great-Uncle Solomon stared for a moment. "I knew it! The ark was real!"

"Of course it was," said Peter. "You just need to trust God."

Mary looked out the window. "Hey, it stopped raining."

Hank ran and got his ball to play.

"Let's go outside," said Great-Uncle Solomon.

They walked out the front door.

Peter pointed in the sky. "Look! There's a rainbow!" He smiled as he thought of Noah and his family seeing the first rainbow in the sky.

Peter looked at Mary. He wondered where their next adventure would take them.

Do you want to read more about the events in this story?

The people, places, and events in *Race to the Ark* are drawn from stories in the Bible. You can read more about them in the following passages of the Bible.

Genesis chapters 4 and 5 tell about Noah and his family.

Genesis chapter 6 tells that mankind had become wicked and God instructed Noah to build an ark for his family and the animals.

Genesis chapter 7 describes the forty days of rain and the flood that covered the earth.

Genesis chapter 8 tells about the earth drying up and Noah and his family and the animals leaving the ark.

Genesis chapter 9 says that God placed a rainbow in the sky as a sign of his promise to never again flood the earth.

CATCH ALL
PETER AND MARY'S ADVENTURES!

In ***The Beginning,*** Peter, Mary, and Hank witness the Creation of the earth while battling a sneaky snake.

In ***The Great Escape,*** Peter, Mary, and Hank journey to Egypt and see the devastation of the plagues.

In ***Journey to Jericho,*** the trio lands in Jericho as the Israelites prepare to enter the Promised Land.

In ***The Shepherd's Stone,*** Peter, Mary, and Hank accompany David as he prepares to fight Goliath.

In ***The Lion's Roar,*** the trio arrive in Babylon and uncover a plot to get Daniel thrown in the lions' den.

In ***The King Is Born,*** Peter, Mary, and Hank visit Bethlehem at the time of Jesus' birth.

ABOUT THE AUTHOR

Mike Thomas grew up in Florida playing sports and riding his bike to the library and the arcade. He graduated from Liberty University, where he earned a bachelor's degree in Bible Studies.

When his son Peter was nine years old, Mike went searching for books that would teach Peter about the Bible in a fun and imaginative way. Finding none, he decided to write his own series. In The Secret of the Hidden Scrolls, Mike combines biblical accuracy with adventure, imagination, and characters who are dear to his heart. The main characters are named after Mike's son Peter, his niece Mary, and his dog, Hank.

Mike lives in Tennessee with his wife, Lori; two sons, Payton and Peter; and Hank.

For more information about the author and the series, visit www.secretofthehiddenscrolls.com.